Life inside a laboratory breeding facility is hard. The place is a factory. Living, breathing, thinking individuals are its products. These products are produced, modified and manipulated to order before being sent to customers who will subject them to even worse ordeals.

Is there any chance of escape from such a place? Almost never, but Hugo is the one-in-a-million who made it out. This is his story.

Let the dogs out is fiction. Any resemblance to people, companies, circumstances or events in real life is *not* coincidental.

little-chicken.net

"I believe I am not interested to know whether Vivisection produces results that are profitable to the human race or doesn't. To know that the results are profitable to the race would not remove my hostility to it. The pains which it inflicts upon unconsenting animals is the basis of my enmity towards it, and it is to me sufficient justification of the enmity without looking further."

Mark Twain

in a letter to the London Anti-Vivisection Society,

May 26, 1899

With love and thanks to my dear friend, EB,
without whom this story would not have been painted.

VP

Let the dogs out was first shared online in 2012
at violetsvegancomics.com

Second edition published in Great Britain in April 2018

This edition published in 2024
by Little Chicken Books
Scarborough, North Yorkshire, England
little-chicken.net

A CIP catalogue record for this book is available
from the British Library

ISBN 978-1-7385597-2-5

Many thanks to the creators and distributors of the fonts
used in the illustrations,
downloaded from fontsquirrel.com and dafont.com:

Kingthings Trypewriter 2 by Kevin King of
kingthingsfonts.co.uk
AFTER SHOK by Dave Kellam and Brian Stuparyk
Rabiohead by Jakob Fischer of pizzadude.dk
SH Pinscher by Tinghao Hu of behance.net/says-hu
ARMALITE RIFLE by Vic Fieger of vicfieger.com
Bombadier by Apostrophic Labs
and Rage Italic by Ron Zwingelberg used on the front cover

Let the dogs out

by Violet Plum

Little Chicken Books
Scarborough * North Yorkshire * England
little-chicken.net

Yep, life is good,
though it wasn't
always. I've been
extremely lucky but
I haven't forgotten
those who weren't.
Listen very
carefully,
I'm going
to tell you
a story ...

A year ago I was huddled on a sawdust-covered concrete floor with my three brothers.

Our worn-out mother hardly looked at us. We wanted to be close to her but she was distant. I didn't understand it then but now I know she was exhausted and without hope. Her eyes had no spark left in them.

Where we lived there were many families like ours. So many.
The noise was constant: barking, yelping,howling. And the stink! You can imagine.

One of my earliest memories is of three bipeds going to the cage opposite ours. They hesitated before unlocking it because the mum who lived there started going mad. She was growling and snarling and barking. She did not want them there!

One of the bipeds opened the gate carefully so that another, holding a long stick, could move in. As it did so, the mother moved in front of her pups and snarled a fierce warning at the intruder. In an instant the biped used the stick to pin her against the wall while another one entered the pen.

There was nothing she could do.

They added her puppies to the others in their trolley.

After that she just howled and howled.
For the whole day I watched, waiting for them to come back. They never did.
My mum just sat by our gate and her eyes glazed over as she stared in the direction of the other mother
who howled all day.

I was scared. I kept seeing the same thing happening again and again over the next few weeks, until it was our turn, mine and my brother's.
The bipeds came for us.

They opened our gate and stepped inside. My mum just laid down in front of us and whimpered. I don't think she had any fight left in her, or else she just knew resistance was futile.

One of them pushed her out of the way with the side of its foot so that they could get what they came for.

Only two of us were chosen.

We were taken to two other bipeds in a
smaller, quieter room.

I could see more like us, caged alone
against the opposite wall.

There was a strange and sickly smell.

OKAY, THIS IS THE FIRST THING YOU'VE GOT TO LEARN AS AN ANIMAL TECHNICIAN. THESE GUYS ARE NOT USED TO BEING HANDLED SO YOU'VE GOT TO GET THEM USED TO IT. HOLD THEM FIRMLY AND SECURELY AND TEACH THEM TO BEHAVE.
BEHAVE?
CERTAINLY. THEY COULD BE USED IN ORAL TOXICITY TESTS WHERE THEY'LL BE REQUIRED TO SWALLOW DRUGS OR TOXIC SUBSTANCES; THEY MIGHT BE USED FOR DERMAL TOXICITY TESTS FOR WHICH THEY'LL HAVE IRRITATING SUBSTANCES RUBBED INTO THEIR SHAVED SKIN; THEY MIGHT HAVE TO HAVE INJECTIONS, STITCHES, SURGERY, ... WELL, YOU GET THE IDEA. WE HAVE TO ENSURE THEY ARE PLACID AND COOPERATIVE - NOBODY WANTS TO GET BIT.

One of them lifted me onto the table
and held me tight. I tried to
wriggle out of its grasp but it
was too strong.
I couldn't get away. I was so scared.
I growled at it, as fierce as I
could. I was prepared to bite if I
had to but I didn't want a fight -
it was a lot bigger than me.

It wouldn't let go and I started to panic. I barked and barked, telling it to let go of me, but that was a mistake.

It got really angry.

WHAT THE ...? YOU CAN'T TREAT ANIMALS LIKE THAT! I'M GOING TO REPORT THIS!
SHARPS
DANGER
CLINICAL WASTE
BIOHAZARD

IS THAT RIGHT? PERHAPS YOU SHOULD MEET THE LAST PERSON WHO REPORTED ME .... OH, NO, YOU CAN'T, HE DOESN'T WORK HERE ANY MORE.
I'M SORRY ... I JUST .... THAT POOR PUP, HE WAS JUST SCARED THAT'S ALL, YOU DIDN'T NEED TO HIT HIM.
FIRE
YOU'RE VERY OPINIONATED CONSIDERING IT'S YOUR FIRST DAY. CAREFUL NOT TO MAKE IT YOUR LAST.
PUT IT BACK ON THE TABLE AND HOLD ITS EAR BACK, I'VE GOT TO DO ITS TATTOO.
AND HOLD IT STILL!
IN THE INDUCTION THEY TOLD US ....
TATTOO?

One of them held me while the other one did something to the inside of my ear. It scratched me and felt sore but I couldn't lick it. I watched them do the same to my brother and he cried but I couldn't lick his wound either because they shut us in different cages. I felt so frightened and alone.

What happened next was even worse. Another biped came into the room carrying my smaller brothers and leading my mum. One by one they drained the life out of them on the table in front of us.

Eventually they moved us to another cage in another part of the building. There were others about our age who looked as scared and confused as we were. The cage was bigger than we'd been used to but it had the same metal bars, the same concrete floor and the same meagre scattering of sawdust to soak up the mess.

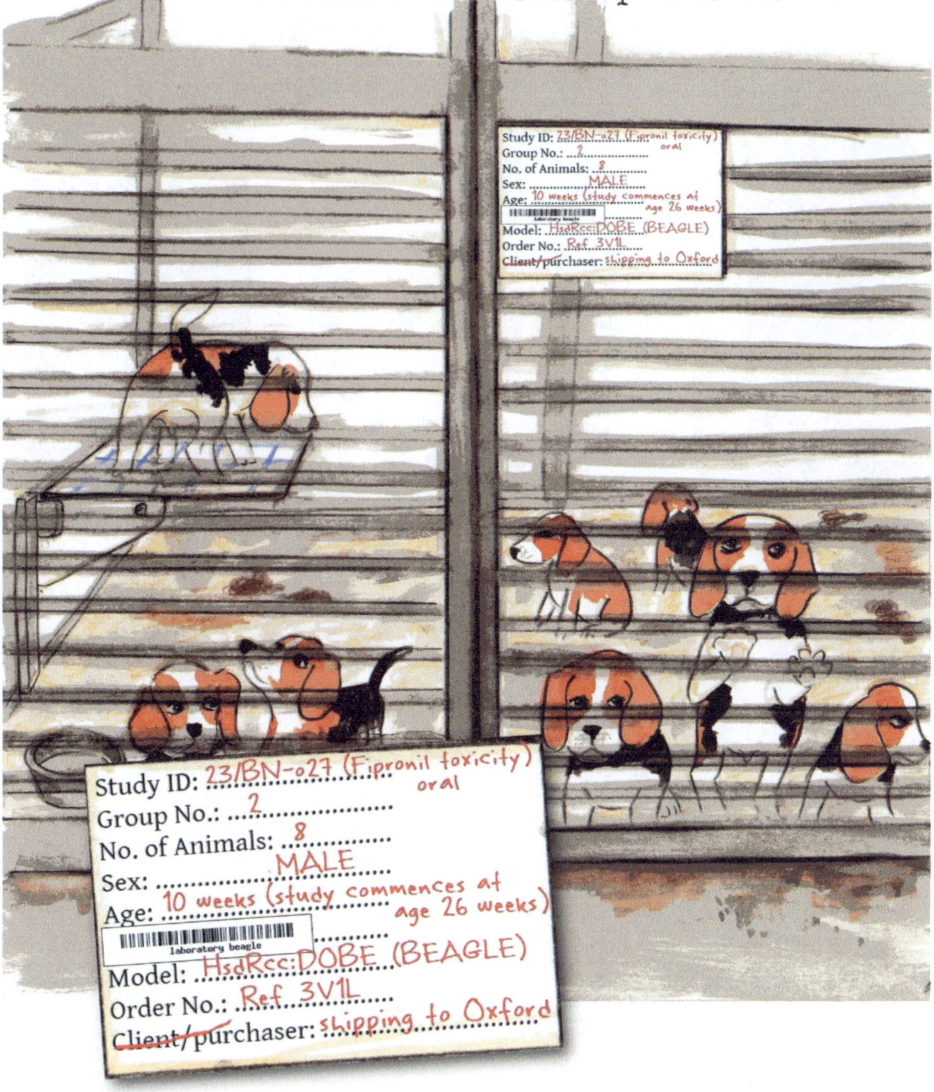

Not long after we were left in this new cage the biped activity stopped. Suddenly it was just us. We could hear other dogs nearby in other cages - lots and lots of them, but no bipeds. We dreaded their return but were strangely not comforted by their absence. Then the lights went out. They went out at the same time every day. It was dark, and all we could do was wait.
ON
OFF
12:00
06:00
18:03
18:00
00:00
MENU
SET
RL60X: INDUSTRIAL LIGHTING TIMER

For a long time after that every day was the same. Nothing happened at first when the lights came back on, but eventually the bipeds would return and peer at us through the bars. They let us play between the cages for a few minutes while they swept out the dirty sawdust and replaced it with clean. Then it was back to our cage for another dreary anxious day.

The weeks dragged by slowly. Bipeds swept up and fed us once a day but apart from that they never entered our cage. Our days were endlessly monotonous but at the same time there was an atmosphere of impending doom. We frequently saw dogs from other cages being carried away and when they returned, if they returned, they looked like they'd been through a horrible ordeal.

YOU'RE NOT SUPPOSED TO CARRY THEM LIKE THAT. YOU SHOULD SUPPORT THEM FROM UNDERNEATH AND HOLD THEM CLOSE TO YOU.
YEAH, WHATEVER

Sometimes, owing to frustration,
desperation and maddening boredom,
there were vicious, bloody fights.

For safety and comfort, my brother and I
stuck close together, day and night.
We were the lucky ones.

Others were so starved of comfort and affection that they rubbed their noses raw against the hard metal as they pushed their faces between the bars trying to reach out to the bipeds when they walked past.

Nine times out of ten they were ignored.

Even worse off were those who were confined alone in a row of small cages opposite ours. Their permanently-shaved forelegs were covered in sore marks and bruises and they never got out of their cages. Once a week a biped would stick a needle in their legs and take blood. They were so used to it that they put up no resistance. When a biped opened their cage they just lifted a paw. Goodness knows how long they'd been there.

SOLITARY

So the days and weeks went slowly by. Dogs came and went. Some stayed a long time, others left the next day. We never knew where they went and we never saw them again.

Each day filled us with dread. Each day we wished it would finally be our turn to leave that horrible place but at the same time were relieved when someone else was chosen.

The thing my brother and I dreaded the most was being separated so I'll never forget everything that happened the last day I saw him.

That day, in the early hours just before dawn, there was a fight, the worst I'd ever seen. By the time the bipeds got there it was way too late. Both fighters were torn, bloody and barely alive. It was a mess. A gory, harrowing mess.

[NACWO: Named Animal Care and Welfare Officer]

We watched as the bloody adversaries were given the needle. Their whimpering stopped. Their breathing slowed.
In moments they were dead.

After that the bipeds cleaned up. They put the bodies into the waste bag
along with the other rubbish.

Almost as soon as they left,
two more bipeds turned up
with some individual cages on wheels.

When the cages' wheels wobbled to a stand-still, a piece of paper slid off the top and glided to the ground. The way one biped studied it when he picked it up led me to suspect that it was key to what was going to happen to us.

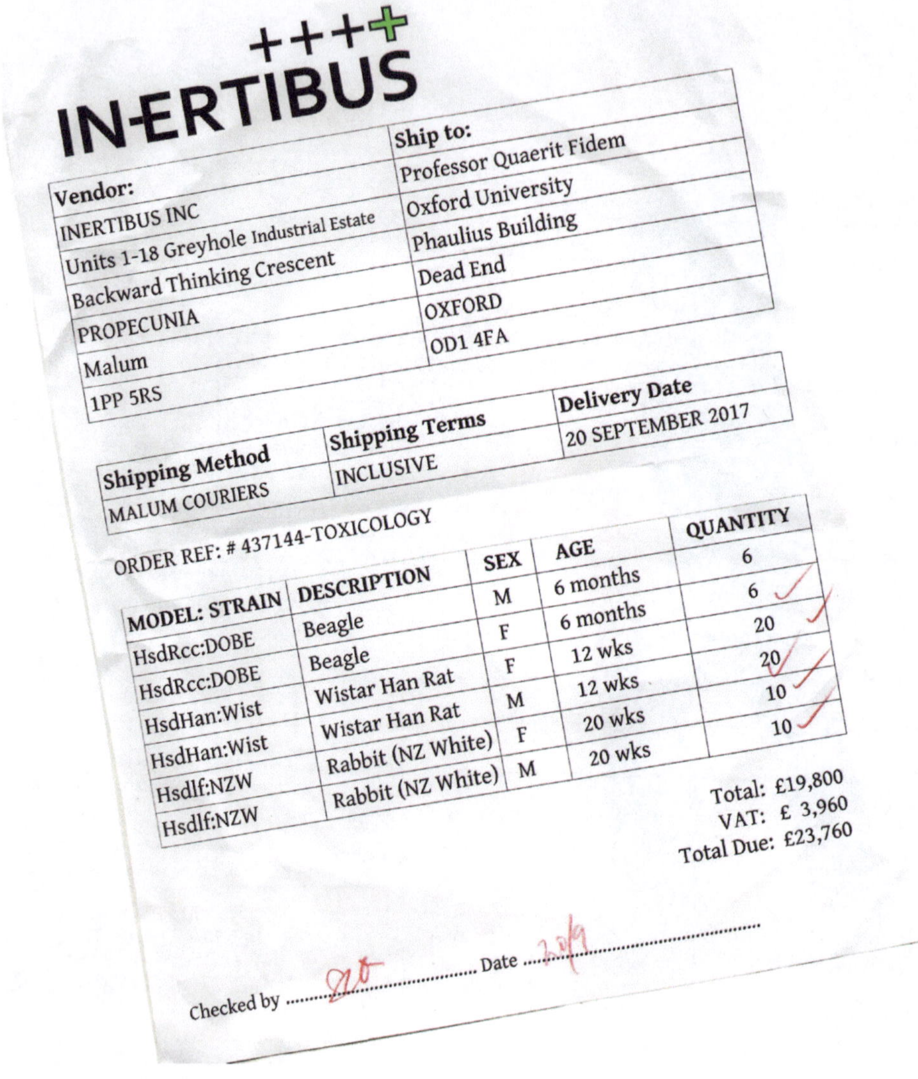

INERTIBUS

Vendor:	Ship to:
INERTIBUS INC	Professor Quaerit Fidem
Units 1-18 Greyhole Industrial Estate	Oxford University
Backward Thinking Crescent	Phaulius Building
PROPECUNIA	Dead End
Malum	OXFORD
1PP 5RS	OD1 4FA

Shipping Method	Shipping Terms	Delivery Date
MALUM COURIERS	INCLUSIVE	20 SEPTEMBER 2017

ORDER REF: # 437144-TOXICOLOGY

MODEL: STRAIN	DESCRIPTION	SEX	AGE	QUANTITY
HsdRcc:DOBE	Beagle	M	6 months	6
HsdRcc:DOBE	Beagle	F	6 months	6 ✓
HsdHan:Wist	Wistar Han Rat	F	12 wks	20 ✓
HsdHan:Wist	Wistar Han Rat	M	12 wks	20 ✓
Hsdlf:NZW	Rabbit (NZ White)	F	20 wks	10 ✓
Hsdlf:NZW	Rabbit (NZ White)	M	20 wks	10 ✓

Total: £19,800
VAT: £ 3,960
Total Due: £23,760

Checked by ...... Date 20/9

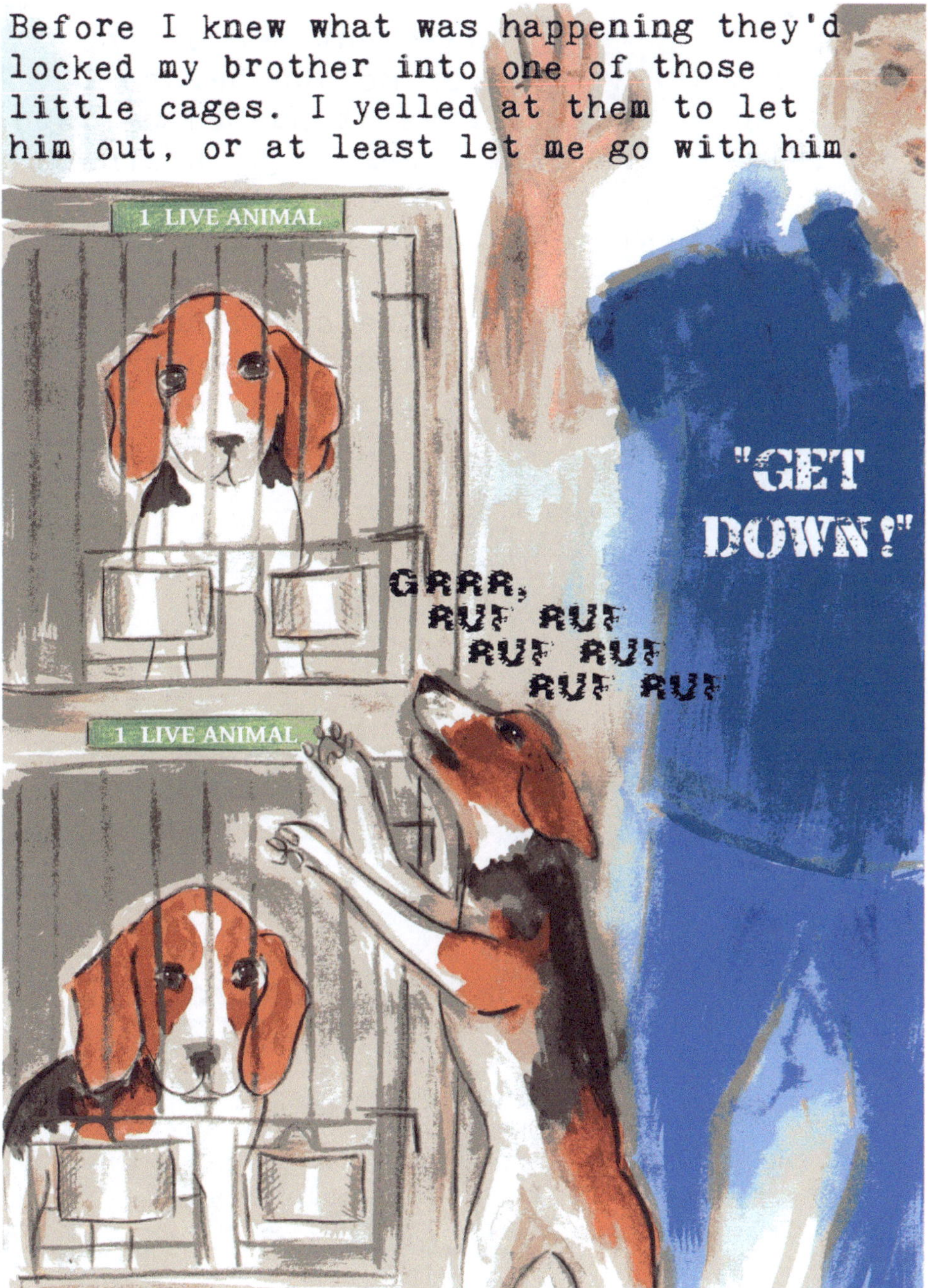
Before I knew what was happening they'd locked my brother into one of those little cages. I yelled at them to let him out, or at least let me go with him.
1 LIVE ANIMAL
"GET DOWN!"
GRRR,
RUF RUF
RUF RUF
RUF RUF
1 LIVE ANIMAL

I tried to jump up again but one of the bipeds grabbed hold of me and before I could wriggle free it pushed me into another of the little cages. My brother and I called out to each other and desperately pleaded to be reunited but they took no notice.

All we could hope for was that we were going to the same place.

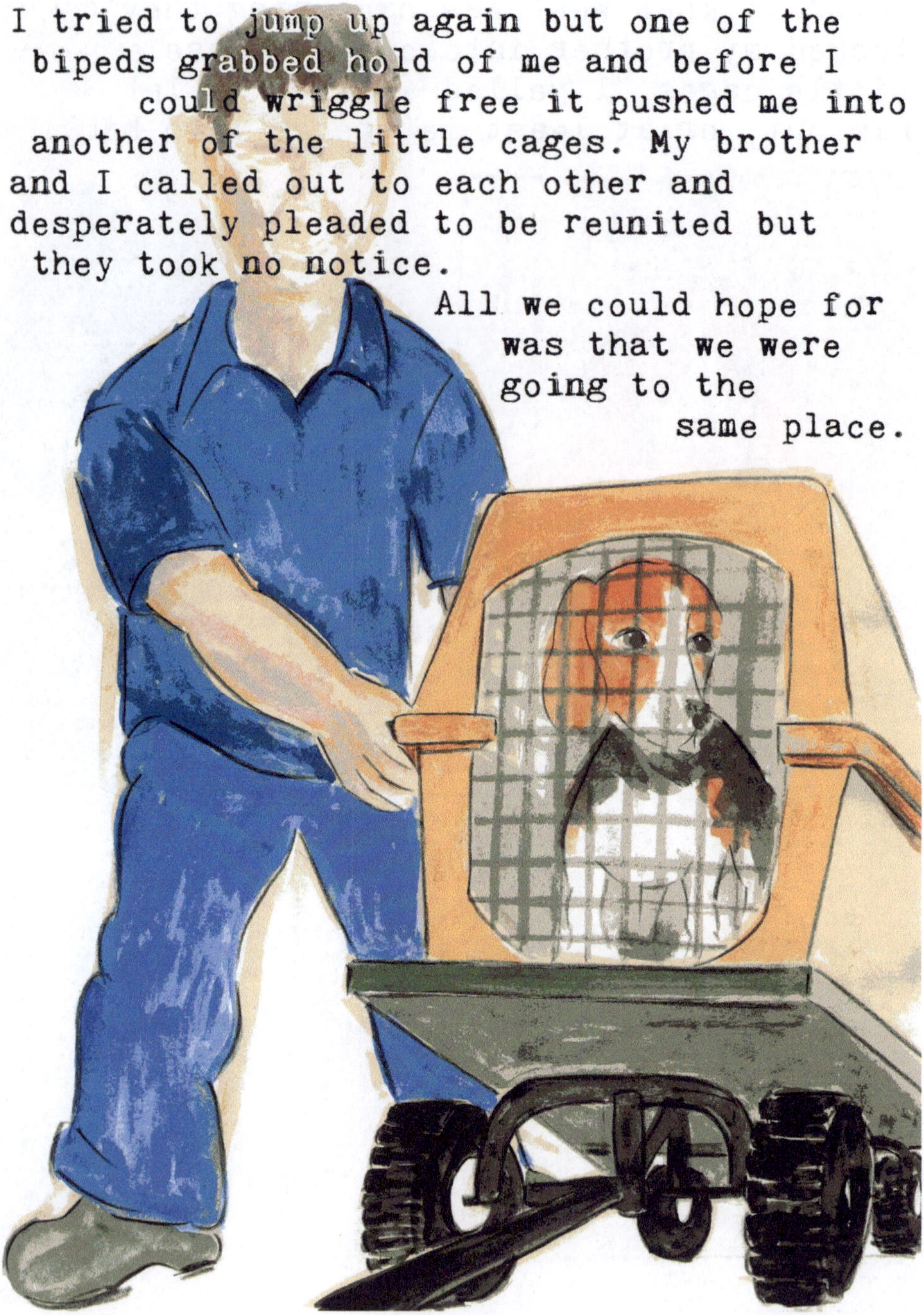

The bipeds wheeled the cages down a long, cold corridor towards a bright light. I kept my eyes firmly fixed on my brother's cage in front of me, terrified I'd lose sight of him. Suddenly the air smelled cleaner. A breeze brushed my face, bringing with it a hundred new smells. But I knew I couldn't afford to be distracted. I strained for a glimpse of my brother, briefly catching his eye when they turned his cage to load it onto the waiting white van.

I was last to be put into the van and my cage faced away from everyone else so I couldn't see my brother. I couldn't see any of the others but I could smell them and they smelled terrified.

OKAY, IT'S ALL LOCKED UP AT THE BACK SO YOU'RE GOOD TO GO!
INERTIBUS
Certified Testing Laboratory & Breeding Facility
CHEERS MATE. SEE YA NEXT TIME!

As the van pulled away all I could think was - No No No! My brother my brother! I had no idea what was happening but I was so so scared. For him and for me.

From the way the cage rattled and jolted
  I knew we were in a hurry.
Fear and confusion kept me quiet.

OKAY BOY, THIS IS IT. LET'S HOPE WE CAN GET THROUGH THE GATE BY HANGING ON TO HIS COAT TAILS. "MAY FORTUNE FAVOUR THE FOOLISH."
HOW'S MY DRIVING? CALL 0800 SLAVE TRADER
OFF2 KIL
WED
11:58
20:09:17
The Shins
Oh Inverte...
Track 02

It was only then that I realised which biped this was. This one was different from the rest. It had been gentle and kind. It had spoken softly to us and intervened when others were rough. I knew then that it meant me no harm.

But very soon ....

We started going faster - too fast.
My cage rattled from side to side.
I felt sick.

FIRST WE NEED TO GET OUT OF SIGHT.
WE NEED SOMEWHERE TO HIDE.
FR33 NOW
OH YES! THAT LOOKS PROMISING!

The biped steered us into a sharp U-turn and then stopped.
GOOD. THAT'S BOUGHT US A BIT OF TIME. BUT NOT MUCH. C'MON.
POLICE
PC02 PLOD

The biped lifted my cage out of its vehicle and opened it. It clearly wanted me to get out but I was hesitant. It was all new - the sights, the sounds, the smells - and a little overwhelming. But before long I couldn't resist stepping out. There was a soft, cool, moist, sweet-smelling carpet at my feet and it was exhilarating.

I wondered when the biped would bring my brother here. Soon, I hoped.

What happened next was very strange. I'd never seen or felt such affection from a biped.

It released me from its embrace and patted my back as if telling me to leave. I was unsure at first but soon realised that it was up to me to find my brother. I began to run.

Before I had gone far a noise behind me caused me to stop and look back. Two more bipeds were coming to meet the other one and I was glad I had not waited.

So, I knew I just needed to find
the white van.

And I did.
I kept finding it,
losing it,
finding it again ...

.... and losing it again.

I rested when I had to, ate what I could find. I was so tired and beginning to feel hopeless.
All I could think of was finding my brother and the only lead I had was the white van. I thought if I could just catch the white van ...

Then, just when I had given up hope,
I saw it. Parked. And open.

I didn't hesitate.

I should have known. From the smells alone, I should have known. I sat motionless. Devastated. Trying to face the truth I'd been avoiding for so long. My brother was gone. I would never see him again.

It was a trap!
'ELLO 'ELLO, WHAT'S GOIN' ON 'ERE THEN?
The biped was between me and the open door. I didn't have the nerve to charge towards it so I climbed under one of the shelves and desperately tried to scratch out an escape hole.

But it was no use. Whatever the van was made of was impenetrable to my claws. I could feel the biped touching my back and knew that my freedom was at an end.

I didn't know it yet, but that was the moment everything changed.

From that day on we were almost never out of each other's sight.
It was a strange new world.
Dr Hadwen Trust
ANIMAL FREE
RESEARCH UK
Welcome!
YOU READY FOR THIS HUGO? YOUR FIRST DAY AT WORK! THE STAFF AND CUSTOMERS ARE GONNA LOVE YOU!
I became known by the new name she gave me and everyone I met was kind to me, though I was still me, and they were all bipeds.

I am well fed and well loved; I feel safe
and know I am very very lucky; but the
place I came from will never leave me,

and my heart aches
for my brother
who is with me
only in my dreams.

So, that's my story. My story so far. Thanks for listening.

Background and Sources

This story was originally written in 2012 to support the campaign *Save The Harlan Beagles* and conditions described inside the story's breeding facility are informed by a former Harlan employee's account which was widely publicised at the time.

notoanimalexperiments.com/about-us/save-the-harlan-beagles.html

In 2014 Harlan was acquired by the notorious contract testing laboratory, Huntingdon Life Sciences (HLS)
sourcewatch.org/index.php/Huntingdon_Life_Sciences

so the story has been slightly modified in 2018 to include a little information taken from insider accounts of former employees there. However, very little of this was used because it is too distressing for a children's book.

In 2015 Harlan and HLS together became Envigo - a new name for a fresh start. But a visit to their website in 2018 revealed nothing had actually changed.

envigo.com

The website was clean and fresh, with a slideshow of happy smiling people revolving under the confident claim that they are

Delivering scientific excellence and an outstanding customer experience that helps you secure the potential of life enhancing research and products globally.

I clicked on a tab at random: Pharmaceutical Development

Then a subsection: Pharma Services

I chose from a long list: Discovery Services and Lead Candidate Selection

Then: In Vivo [performed in a living organism]

- Discovery Pharmacology

Under the heading, ***What you can expect***, the website explained:

- Our experience encompasses the use of multiple species including rodents and larger animals, as well as the evaluation of an extremely diverse set of test materials

- We have performed more than 150 efficacy and disease model studies in multiple species for a number of therapeutic targets and we continue to expand our areas of expertise

Our respiratory inflammation services:

- The house dust mite model of chronic allergic inflammation (mouse)
- Antigen-induced pulmonary inflammation (ovalbumin sensitized brown Norway rat, mouse or guinea pig)
- LPS induced non-allergic pulmonary inflammation (mouse, rat, guinea pig; also primate in our US facility)
- Cigarette smoke-induced pulmonary inflammation (mouse)
- Bleomycin-induced lung fibrosis (rat)
- Bronchoconstriction/ bronchodilator studies in conscious and anesthetized animals (rodent, guinea pig and dog)
- All standard routes of delivery available
- Inhalation delivery optional
  - ➢ Aerosol and dry powder
  - ➢ Unique in-house developed system for dry powder delivery

Our gastrointestinal services:

- Emesis / anti-emesis (ferret)
- GI motility (rodent; large animal planned for development)
- IBD models (rodent; primate planned for development)
- Feeding / dietary models (rodent)

Our anti-infective services:

- Wound healing (+/- MRSA infection) (rodent, rabbit, pig)
- Influenza - tissue burden and biomarker endpoints
- Host resistance

Our cardiovascular services:

- Heamodynamics and electrocardiology (rodent and large animal)

- Echocardiography in development for rodent and large animals
- Ion channel electrophysiology
- Bioanalysis and biomarker (translational) assessment

I clicked on another tab: Chemical

and a subsection: Reprotoxicology

[reproductive toxicology = study of the adverse effects of substances on the embryo, fetus, neonate and prepubertal mammal and the adult reproductive and neuroendocrine systems.]

Here they offered:

- Study designs for non-pharmaceuticals
- Dosing by all oral (dietary or gavage [the administration of food or drugs by force, especially to an animal, typically through a tube leading down the throat to the stomach]), dermal and inhalation routes
- Fetal pathology including Wilson's sectioning and micro-dissection techniques, staining for bone and cartilage
- Specialist neuropathology and morphometric measurements of the brain
- Specialist pathology of male and female reproductive organs

These are just a couple of examples from a very long list of Envigo services.

"Envigo provides mission-critical products and research services for pharmaceutical, crop protection, and chemical companies as well as universities, governments, and other research organizations," to quote their *About* page.

So that's a tiny glimpse at the former HLS side of things. The former Harlan side of things is what it always was: a supplier of unwilling participants.

They write in their *Contract Breeding and Services* leaflet - "... we aim to be the most dependable supplier of Contract Breeding Services in the industry."

I clicked on the Research Models and Services tab

and the subsection: Browse Research Models

Here I got to choose from 45 different types of mice, eg inbred mice, hybrid mice, aged mice, albino mice, diabetic mice, obese mice, hairless mice, ... the list went on and on.

The stated research uses of these mice are many:

Toxicology, Carcinogenicity, Embryo donors, Oncology, Transplantation, Tumour cell growth, Immunology, Autoimmune disease, Antibody production, teratology [the scientific study of congenital abnormalities and abnormal formations] Metabolism, Cardiovascular, Memory, Osteoarthritis, Neoplasia, Immune response, Longevity, Vision and hearing, Motor skills, Renal degeneration, Age-associated pathology, Neurobiology, Reproductive senescence, Ageing, Background for induced and genetically-modified models, Diet-induced obesity, Superovulation, Behaviour and learning disabilities, Drug addiction, Alcoholism, ... the list goes on.

Further browsing of *Research Models* provided me with the opportunity to order 22 different types of rat, Dunkin hartley guinea pigs, Golden Syrian hamsters and New Zealand White Rabbits.

Curiously there were no larger animals openly offered here. I looked further. When I searched their entire site for "beagle" I found a pdf:

Model Data Sheet: RCC Beagle Dog

Origin

Colony started in 1982 at BRL Biological Research Laboratories Ltd., Switzerland (part of the RCC Group) as a mix of two origins including:

- Kleintierfarm Madörin, Füllinsdorf, Switzerland
- Hazleton Research Products, Kalamazoo, USA

Envigo obtained the colony through acquisition in 2004. Colonies are available in France and the UK.

The same search also brought up two other papers about beagles:

- Development of a chronic pulmonary arterial pressure model in the Beagle dog (Explore the many methods and techniques used when measuring PAP; Consider the challenges that some of these techniques can create using the Beagle dog)

- Development of a neurobehavioral, cardiovascular, and respiratory (NCR) assessment methodology using orally administered amphetamine and acepromazine in conscious Beagle dogs

A search for "fish" revealed a lot of information about fish as part of the diets of other research animals (including primates, guinea pigs and pigs) as well as this paper:

- Pitfalls in law-abiding long-term fish toxicity testing instead of short-term to reduce animal consumption which explains how to abide by the law when testing pharmaceuticals (Medicinal Products for Human Use) and other substances on fish.

A search for "avian" produced:

- Ecotoxicology

Whether you are focused on aquatic, avian, or terrestrial toxicology, your goal is to quickly and confidently determine if your product is safe. ... As your partner, we offer you access to our state-of-the-art facilities including our purpose-built avian facility with incubation room and hatchery, our high-spec aquatic toxicology facilities, and our outdoor facility which incorporates 32ft2 microcosms and more than 60 ditch units.

Our knowledge and expertise in ecotoxicology is backed by 1000 terrestrial studies conducted in the last six years alone, including almost 200 avian studies.

This is business as usual at Envigo. Nothing but the name has changed.

So what can we do?

Though there are a great many of us who believe, as Mark Twain did, that there is not, nor could there ever be, any justification for vivisection, it must be acknowledged that if it were possible to stop it by campaigning on grounds of cruelty to animals, it would have been stopped a century ago.

I believe the most effective way to consign vivisection to the history books is by campaigning on scientific grounds.

"True advances in medical knowledge have not come from animals. When, on rare occasion, advances took place through animal experimentation, they were not *incumbent* on animals. Alternative methods - autopsies, *in vitro* research, clinical observation, epidemiology, mathematical modeling, and other human-based research modalities - could have resulted in the same achievements without injury to humans. Animal models are inaccurate, superfluous, and create risk to humans."

from *Sacred Cows and Golden Geese* by Ray Greek MD and Jean Swingle Greek DVM

Support organisations fighting this corner:

➔ The Physicians' Committee for Responsible Medicine

pcrm.org

The Physicians Committee is leading a revolution in medicine - putting a new focus on health and compassion. The Physicians Committee combines the clout and expertise of more than 12,000 physicians with the dedicated actions of more than 175,000 members across the United States and around the world.

pcrm.org/about-us

PCRM employs highly qualified Research Issues Experts who work tirelessly for higher standards in human research; for alternatives to animal research; and to modernize drug development to save human and animal lives by shifting preclinical research from the use of animals to modern technologies that are more relevant to human biology.

PCRM also enables you to be the best animal advocate you can be by educating yourself about animal experimentation. They provide literature which can be downloaded.

➔ Safer Medicines

safermedicines.org

Safer Medicines Campaign is an independent patient safety organisation of scientists and doctors with extensive expertise in drug development. Our aim is to change the way medicines are tested, so they are safer for humans: moving from a system based mainly on tests on animals to one focused firmly on human biology. Adverse drug reactions kill 197,000 people in the EU every year and more than 100,000 in the US. The time for action is NOW!

It is often claimed that scientists and doctors are united in their belief in the value of, and necessity for, animal experiments to protect human health [but] there has been a long tradition of scepticism about this issue.

Many factors perpetuate animal research, the most obvious of which is tradition. The animal research paradigm is very deeply embedded within research institutions. Laboratories, researchers' careers, technologies, publication practices and funding streams are now 'locked-in' to the paradigm. For example, it is easier and faster to publish papers based on animal research than on human research, and a good publication record will attract funding to continue that research.

Money Money Money

Pharmaceutical companies continue to do animal tests because regulators require them to do so and because (despite their lack of reliability) animal tests provide liability protection in court when drugs injure or kill people. Yet most of the animal tests accepted by regulators have never been validated.

When polio first appeared around 1835, it rapidly paralysed and killed its victims. In 1908, a virus was suspected and scientists began working on a vaccine. They discovered the polio virus in human intestines as early as 1912, suggesting entrance through the digestive tract. However, because animal research indicated that monkeys contract polio nasally, and because scientists working on the vaccine ignored the human findings in favour of the animal findings, the development of an effective vaccine was postponed for decades. In 1941, after conducting human autopsies, Dr. Albert Sabin found the virus confined to the gastrointestinal tract as had been documented nearly 30 years earlier. He noted that 'prevention was long delayed by the erroneous conception of the nature of the human disease based on misleading experimental models of the disease in monkeys.' (Sabin 1984)

Go to safermedicines.org/page/resources to find printed materials, audio visual archive, articles and reports, published letters, a list of useful websites, FAQs, medical research in the news, the Safer Medicines film, and Conference presentations.

And an organisation which exclusively funds biomedical research and testing without animals:

➔ The Dr Hadwen Trust: Animal Free Research UK

animalfreeresearchuk.org

Since 1970, we have awarded grants to over 260 projects. These include research into cancer, Alzheimer's disease, asthma, diabetes, kidney, heart and liver disease, to name only a few. We are consulted internationally for our expertise in animal replacement science and we sit on several government and non-governmental bodies in order to advance animal free research.

animalfreeresearchuk.org/our-impact/

*

Make sure you're not funding vivisection

It's important to be aware that some well-known medical charities commission vivisection and if you donate to them your money may be funding cruel and pointless animal experiments. Before donating to a charity, find out whether they fund vivisection by writing to them. Don't be satisfied with the assurances of the nice ladies behind the till at the charity shop, write to Head Office.

Animal Aid provides a comprehensive list of good and bad charities:

https://www.victimsofcharity.org/

but, because sometimes charities' policies change, they ask people to please contact them after receiving a reply from a charity about their animal testing policy, so that they can keep their list up to date. They also explain that some charities may not be directly involved in animal research but are members of the *Association of Medical Research Charities* (AMRC). This is an organisation that promotes the use of animals in laboratories and currently requires its members to support the practice of vivisection.

You can order a free wallet-sized printed copy of the list from Animal Aid or get the Cruelty-Free Giving app for your phone.

We must fight for a change in the law

Many vivisectors use the excuse that "... many of the dogs used are for toxicology safety studies. These are required by law. Any new medicine has to be tested in both rodents, usually rats, and a larger non-rodent mammal, usually dogs, before it can legally be given to human volunteers."

quote taken from *The Daily Express* exposé in 2013 of the British Heart Foundation's experiments on dogs – https://www.express.co.uk/news/uk/425965/EXCLUSIVE-Outrage-as-major-UK-charity-uses-donations-to-fund-vivisection-tests-on-dogs

This in itself proves how unscientific vivisection is. A contract testing laboratory's job is to get approval for a particular drug or chemical and they do this by testing it on different species until they find one that gives them the desired result. If tests on rabbits show it to be unsafe, they can test it on cats, dogs, pigs, monkeys, ... until they produce the result they're looking for.

For example, in 2018, I visited

envigo.com/products-services/chemical/inhalation-toxicology/

to discover that the species available for Inhalation Toxicology at Envigo were Rat, Mouse, Dog, Rabbit, Guinea Pig, Hamster, Mini Pig, Pygmy Goat or Cow. They confidently promised -

"Tell us your challenge and then we'll work with you to choose the appropriate solution."

*

Envigo's website has changed again since then as, in 2019, Covance (another contract research company) bought Envigo's non-clinical* research service business, while Envigo's Research Models Services business bought the Covance Research Products business. It's all the same to the animals.

*non-clinical study = A generic term for any study - e.g., biochemical, Drosophila, rodent, etc. - not performed on human subjects.

BV - #0015 - 160924 - C72 - 229/152/4 - PB - 9781738559725 - Matt Lamination